The Dog Detectives in...
An Outback Odyssey

Fin & Zoa

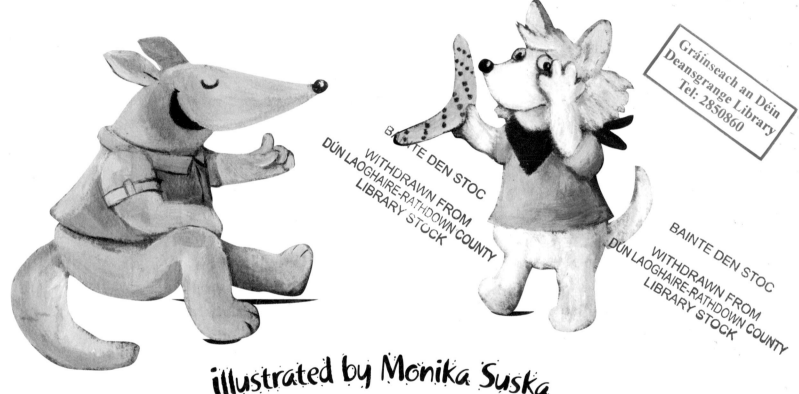

illustrated by Monika Suska

Detective Jack and Deputy Poco Loco are cycling through the hot, dry Australian Outback when they crash into a new case. A group of dirty and devious dingoes have stolen a very special didgeridoo and it's up to the Dog Detectives to sniff out their trail.

In the sunburnt scrub beyond the Bottlebrush trees is the Australian Outback, a place far from the seas. It's hot and it's dry and it has lots of flies, but it's the dark of the night that the dingoes despise.

In the dark of their den the dingoes doze, they toss and they turn
and they itch at their toes. No one is sure, the reason's unknown,
why they're cursed with nightmares deep in their bones.

Nothing helps, neither lullabies nor lotions, not even super-strength
eucalyptus potions.

One night a tired and sleepless dingo sat under the glow of the moonlight hurling

rocks at the moon when...

"Hey! That was my house you just threw away!" A blue tongued

lizard shouted, sticking out his long blue tongue.

"You know some of us are trying to sleep!"

"Lucky for you," grumbled the dingo.
"Nothing will stop my nightmares."
"Nightmares?" asked the blue tongued lizard.
"Have you tried music?"

The next evening the dingoes searched the Outback until they found the glow of a campfire. Then they heard the sound of a very unusual musical instrument. One by one the dingoes became enchanted by the soothing hum of the didgeridoo and drifted into dreams.

They snored and snored and snored some more, until they had snored all the way till nine-twenty four.

Meanwhile the Dog Detectives, Detective Jack and Deputy Poco Loco, were racing an emu across the hot, red Australian Outback...

...when suddenly with a whizzzzzzzzzzz and a POP they came to a stop.

"Crikey!" cried Jack "we have a flat tyre."

"Sorry about my boomerang," came a voice from the bushes.

"I thought you were the devious dingoes who stole our didgeridoo."

"Didgeri-who?" asked Jack.
"It's a musical instrument that is sacred to us. It's long like a giant straw and we need it for our ceremony tonight."
"It's your lucky day. We will sniff out your didgeri-donut in no time."

While the Dog Detectives were repairing their tyre under the shade
of a Bottle tree, they heard an enormous laugh from above.
"Koo-ka-ka-ka-ka-kaa-kaaa-kaaaaa-kaaaaaa-ka.
G'day! My name is Katie the Koo-koo-koo-Kookaburra,"
she said with a hiccupping chuckle.

"G'day Katie. Have you seen any didgeri-donut stealing dingoes?" asked Detective Jack, licking his lips.

"Ah, those dirty and devious dingoes!" chuckled Katie the Kookaburra. "They sleep in dens. Keep an eye out for holes in the ground. Come, I'll help you loo-loo-loo-loo-look."

So the team sniffed and searched, from ground and perch until...*sniff sniff sniff*...Deputy Poco Loco's powerful nose found a hole in the ground. Deep in the black hole a pair of beady eyes stared out at them.

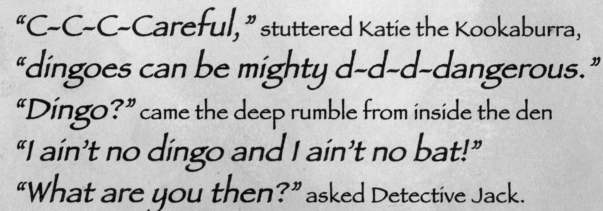

"C-C-C-Careful," stuttered Katie the Kookaburra, *"dingoes can be mighty d-d-d-dangerous."*
"Dingo?" came the deep rumble from inside the den
"I ain't no dingo and I ain't no bat!"
"What are you then?" asked Detective Jack.

Out lumbered a wiry, grey creature with a big, fat belly and short, stubby legs.

"G'day! I'm a Wombat," he said "William K. Wombat to be precise. Pleased to meet you."

"T-T-T-Too slow to be a dingo and t-t-t-too fat to be a bat," cried Katie the Kookaburra with an enormous laugh.

"Hey! Watch it or I'll be cooking a nice juicy Kookaburra pie for dinner," said William K. Wombat. "Now, follow me. I can smell a dirty dingo den from a mile away!"

As William K. Wombat lumbered to a stop, the team heard a horrible spitting and spluttering sound coming from beneath the ground.
"Sounds like the dingoes need some didgeridoo lessons," said Deputy Poco Loco.
"Yeah, sounds more like a didgeri-don't to me," wailed Katie the Kookaburra.

Detective Jack waved the team into a huddle and whispered
"It's time for a plan."

William K. Wombat and the Dog Detectives dug and dug and dug until, with a bubble and a spurt, water exploded out of the ground.

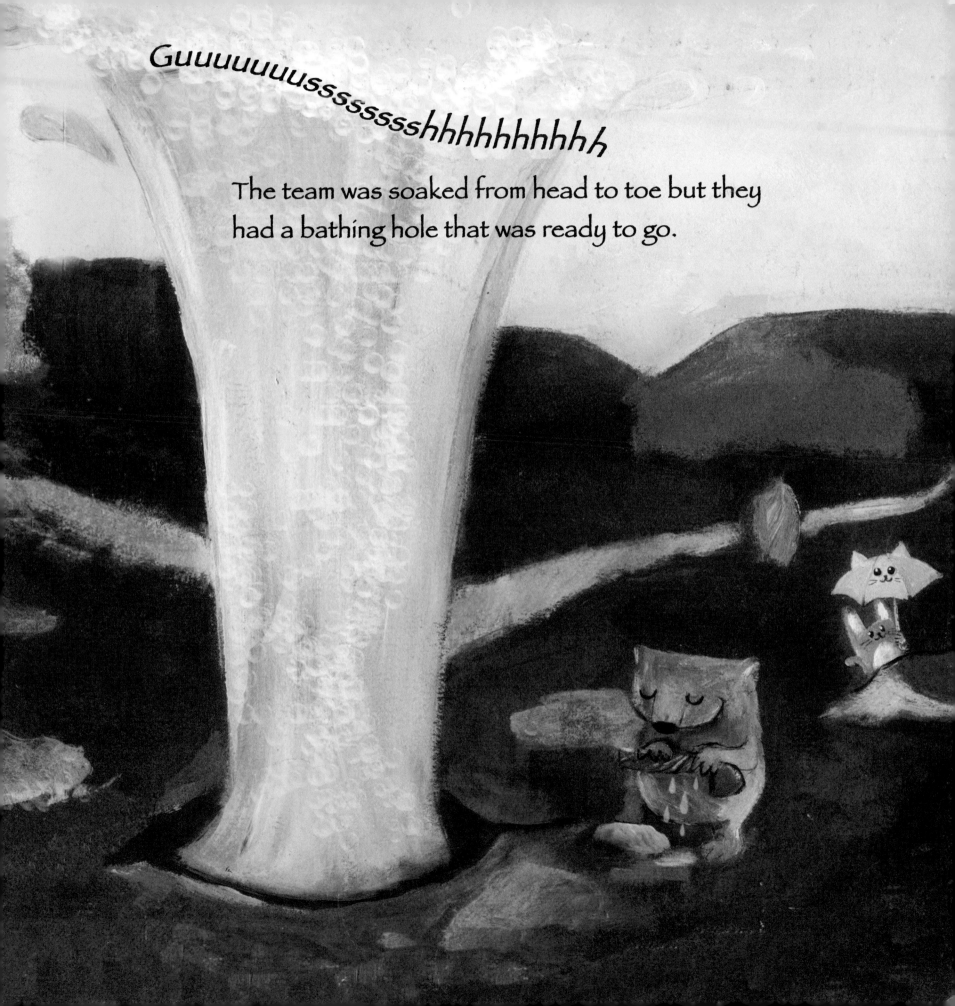

Guuuuuuusssssssshhhhhhhhh

The team was soaked from head to toe but they had a bathing hole that was ready to go.

Soon after the dingoes' didgeridoo practice was interrupted by the loud squawk of Katie the Kookaburra.
"*SPECIAL DELIVERY! SPECIAL DELIVERY!*"

The dingoes ran out to find a paper-bark invitation at their feet.

"*BUBBLIEST BUBBLE BATH EVER,*" one of the dingoes read.

"*I haven't had a bath in years!*" said another dirty dingo.

They all hurried out of the den in search of the bath.

While they splashed and scrubbed, laughed and sang, a dingo noticed the Dog Detectives escaping with the didgeridoo.

He jumped out of the bubble bath and was about to make chase when he looked down and noticed his clean fur was covered in red dirt.

"What's the matter?" his friends asked.

Not wanting to be a dirty dingo again he replied

"Oh nothing," and did a giant belly flop back

into the bubble bath.

The brave team returned the didgeridoo to its grateful owners.
"Thank you Dog Detectives. Why don't you come and share some bush tucker around the fire? We have fresh roasted witchity grubs ready to eat."

"Which grubs?" asked Detective Jack rubbing his belly.
"Witchity grubs," said William K. Wombat "They go perfectly with a nice, juicy Kookaburra pie."

Everyone laughed except Katie the Kookaburra who eventually joined in with a loud "Koo-ka-ka-ka-ka-kaa-kaaa-kaaaaa-kaaaaaa-ka."

The next morning the Dog Detectives cycled off into the horizon refreshed and ready for their next adventure.

THE END!

Outback Facts

The Outback is the vast inland of Australia where people are few and far between. The spaces between towns are so far apart that in much of the Outback the doctor comes by aeroplane.
The Outback is mostly dry, but when it rains it can flood badly.

Aboriginal tribes have lived in the Australian Outback for thousands and thousands of years. They are traditionally nomadic, moving from one area to another to hunt and gather food. Aboriginal tribes have different languages and customs. However one custom they share is the painting of their bodies for ceremonies.

 Didgeridoos are the sacred musical instruments of Aboriginal Australians. They believe the droning sound of the didgeridoo is like the sound of the Outback - the call of an emu, a clap of thunder or a creak of a tree.

 Dingoes are wild dogs that roam great distances and communicate with wolf-like howls. Dingoes are the reason for the longest fence in the world, which stretches across Australia in an attempt to keep them away from grazing sheep.

Kookaburras are named after their hysterical cackling call. Koo-ka-ka-ka-ka-kaa-kaaa-kaaaaa-kaaaaaa-ka. They are territorial birds that nest in tree holes.

Boomerangs are curved throwing sticks traditionally used by Aboriginal Australians for hunting. Some boomerangs can loop back to the thrower if they miss their target.

Witchity Grubs look like fat, white caterpillars and live underground where they feed off the roots of various plants. They can be eaten raw or lightly cooked and are high in protein.

Wombats can move very fast over short distances, despite their appearance! They conserve energy and water to survive droughts by sleeping for up to 18 hours a day in their burrows. There are very few Northern Hairy Nosed Wombats remaining in the world.

Blue Tongued Lizards are reptiles with scaly skin and cold blood. They warm themselves by laying in the sunshine, and use the bright colours of their blue tongue and pink mouth to scare away predators.

Eucalyptus Trees are sometimes known as gum trees because any break in the bark results in the sap oozing from the tree trunk. Eucalyptus trees are very common in Australia and are known for the unique aroma that comes from oils in their leaves.

'An Outback Odyssey'
is an original concept by
authors Zoa & Fin

©Dawn Lumsden
Illustrated by Monika Suska
Monika Suska is represented by MSM Studio
www.msmstudio.eu

**PUBLISHED BY MAVERICK ARTS
PUBLISHING LTD**

©Maverick Arts Publishing Limited (2010)

Studio 4
Hardham Mill Park
Pulborough
RH20 1LA
+44(0) 1798 875980

ISBN 978-1-84886-062-9

www.maverickbooks.co.uk